ACKNOWLEDGEMENTS

Thanks to all of my friends at Animal Inc. you guys made this all possible and for that I will always be grateful and appreciative! Bruce Springsteen, Big Country, Rush, U2, Pete Townshend, The Who, Bob Dylan, The Rolling Stones, The Clash, Rancid, Green Day, The Cure, Stan Lee, Bob Kane, Kathy Cochrane, Jeff Jones, Gary Craig, Kenny Greer, (the great) Jimmy Holmstrom, Scott Morrison, Joel Bloom (along with Carmel and Clarence), the Catanzarite Family, Tony Bernard, Ellen S. Abramowitz, Geoff Boucher, Bryant & Barbra Dillon, Kevin Hellions, Ashley Bileau, Troy Brownfield, John Hogan, Josh Christie, Cassie McCown, Jordan DesJardins, Rik Offenberger, Lissette Manning, Rob Patey, Zach Cox, Danielle Hykes, Esq., Anthony Brooks, Esq., Greg Schell, Cindy Himes, Mark Shuttleworth, Karen Ford, Jeff Hill, Andrea Roewe and everyone at Total Hockey, Keith Primeau, the John Challis Foundation and the Mario Lemiuex Foundation. Lastly, the big three - Troy Dye, Terry Nantier and Chris Warner... thank you for your advice and support. Without you three this book would have never gotten off the ground.

Special thanks to Lillian Moloian and the Moloian Family Foundation, Tom Adamich and Stu Siegel... your unwavering support and kindness will always be remembered and cherished.

Very special thanks to Kris Boban for his amazing work on the book's promo video, my team of Joe Pekar, Ed Brisson and Vickie Adair for their creativity, vision and hard work bringing this story to life. It was a long haul my friends, but I wouldn't have wanted to make the journey without you guys by my side. A huge shout out to Tom Cochrane and Andrew Cosby for their back cover quotes, but more importantly for their friendship, inspiration and the kindness extended to me. To my sister Jody Shapiro and my mom Alice Shapiro whose strength and character are second to none...I love you so much.

Extra special thanks to Gina, Sasha and Nikita, I love you three more than anything in the world.

This book is dedicated to the loving and everlasting memory of my dad, Arnold Shapiro (7/21/31 – 11/11/05), John Challis (12/16/89 – 8/19/08) & Clarence Clemons (1/1/42 – 6/18/11)...

"Everything dies, baby that's a fact, but maybe everything that dies someday comes back." Bruce Springsteen "Atlantic City" 1982.

Mi manchi ogni giorno e vi amo il mio buon amico

The Stereotypical Freaks, A Supersonic Storybook Production was filmed on location in Pittsburgh, PA, Orlando, FL, Vancouver, British Columbia, Austin, TX, Los Angeles, CA and Toronto, Ontario.

For more information please log onto www.howardshapiro.net. Please send your comments, questions or feedback to hockeyplayer4life@gmail.com

Please check out my pages on Facebook http://www.facebook.com/hockeyplayer4life and http://www.facebook.com/pages/Howard-Shapiro/296610707017204?ref=ts

Chapter 1
When It Began

RECOMMENDED LISTENING:

"SUBDIVISIONS"
RUSH

"WHEN IT BEGAN"
THE REPLACEMENTS

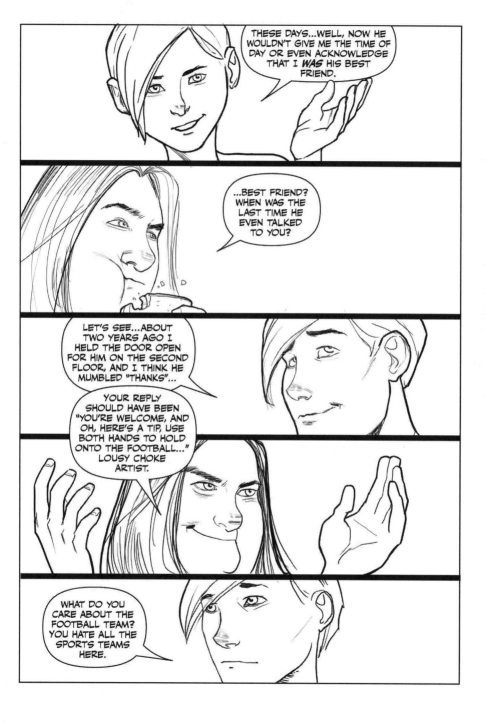

Chapter 2
Jaelithe And Jacoby

I. The Injustice of Fear (Part One)
II. The Future Predecided

RECOMMENDED LISTENING:

"RUBY SOHO"
RANCID

"ON MY WAY HOME"
3

"TIN FOIL"
URGE OVERKILL

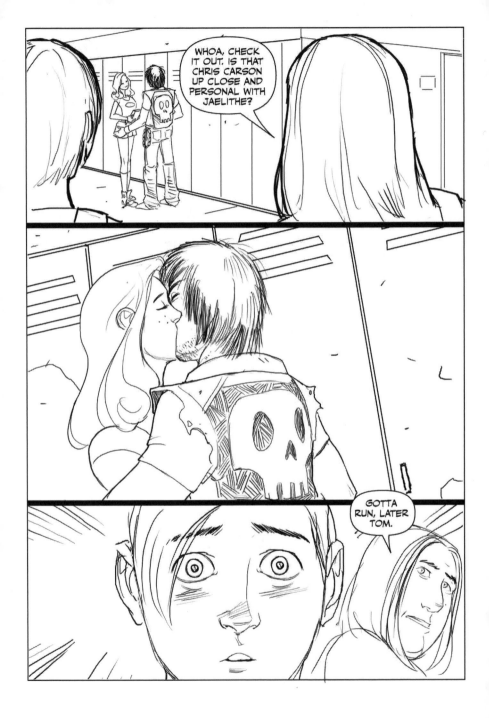

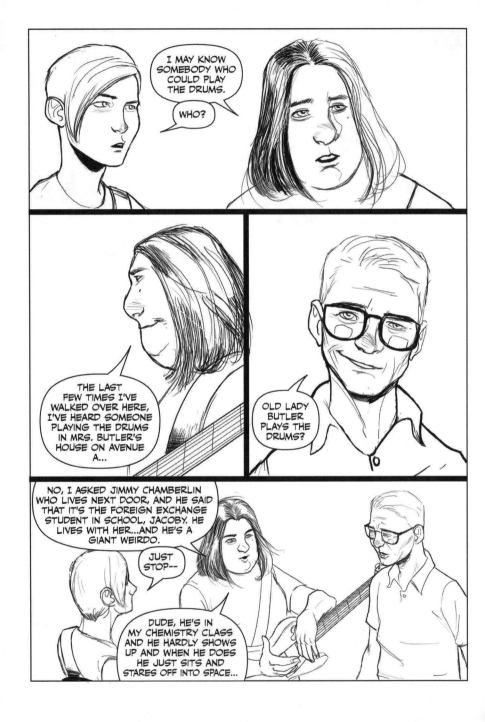

Chapter 3
Reconnection

RECOMMENDED LISTENING:

"TANGLED UP IN BLUE"
BOB DYLAN

"PROMISES BROKEN"
SOUL ASYLUM

THAT WAS WEIRD, BUT IN A GOOD WAY, I GUESS.
I WAS SHOCKED THAT HE WAS THE STUDENT, BUT
I THINK HE WAS EVEN MORE SHOCKED THAT I WAS
THE TUTOR. I'M GLAD WE TALKED ABOUT OUR PAST
FRIENDSHIP. I HAD BUILT UP SO MUCH HOSTILITY AND
ANGER TOWARDS HIM BECAUSE WE WERE SUCH GOOD
FRIENDS. I RECONCILED IT BY THINKING THAT YOU ARE
LUCKY IN LIFE IN YOU HAVE ONE FRIEND LIKE THAT,
SOMEONE YOU TRUST WITH YOUR LIFE. I JUST
HAPPENED TO HAVE A FRIEND LIKE THAT WHEN I
WAS A YOUNG KID... STILL, I CARRIED THAT HURT
AROUND EACH DAY FOR THE LAST FIVE YEARS,
AND IT FELT GOOD TO LET IT GO.

Chapter 4
My Nu Enemy

RECOMMENDED LISTENING:

"BABA O'RILEY"
THE WHO

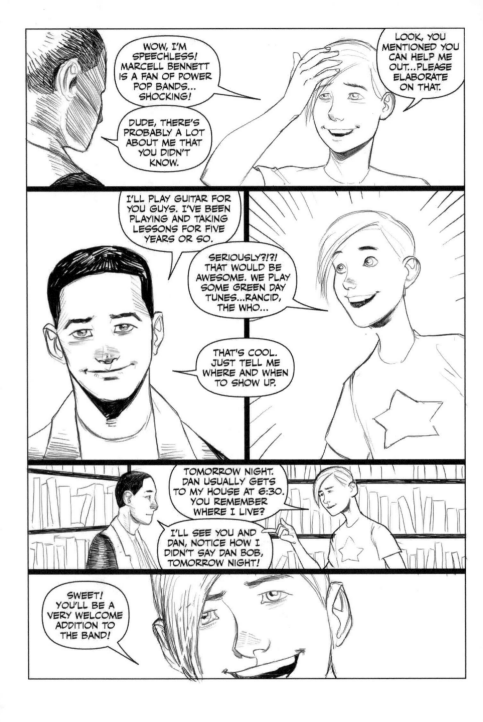

Chapter 5
Befriend Me Now
I. And The Little Man Joined The Band

II. Then They Went 1,2,3,4!!

RECOMMENDED LISTENING:

"GENTLEMEN"
ENTIRE ALBUM BY THE AFGHAN WHIGS

"IN THE EVENING"
LED ZEPPELIN

Chapter 6
Music is the Secret

RECOMMENDED LISTENING:

"JET CITY WOMAN" &
"ANOTHER RAINY NIGHT"
QUEENSRŸCHE

"HOLD ON"
TRIUMPH

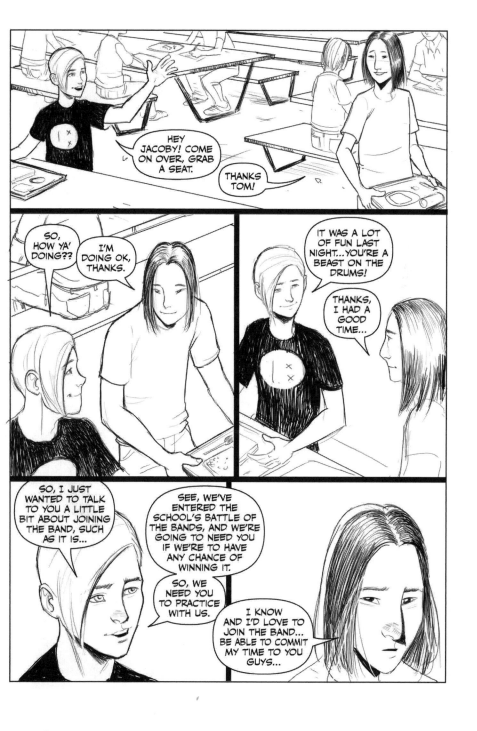

Chapter 7
What it Means
(No Surrender)

RECOMMENDED LISTENING:

"NO SURRENDER"
BRUCE SPRINGSTEEN

"BLOOD BROTHER"
BRUCE SPRINGSTEEN

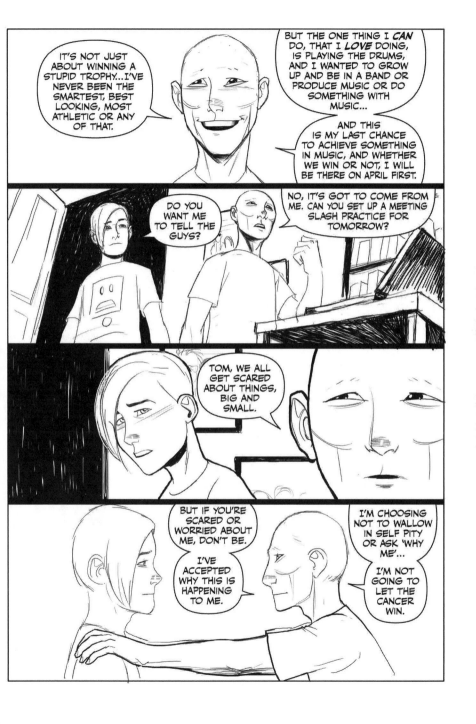

Chapter 8
The Regrets Are Useless

I.   Reflection And Deconstruction
II. A Friend Is A Friend
III. Rise Up

RECOMMENDED LISTENING:

"A FRIEND IS A FRIEND"
PETE TOWNSHEND

Chapter 9
The Persistence Of Timekeeping

RECOMMENDED LISTENING:

"RAVE ON"
BUDDY HOLLY

"I HEAR THE CALL"
THE UNFORGIVEN

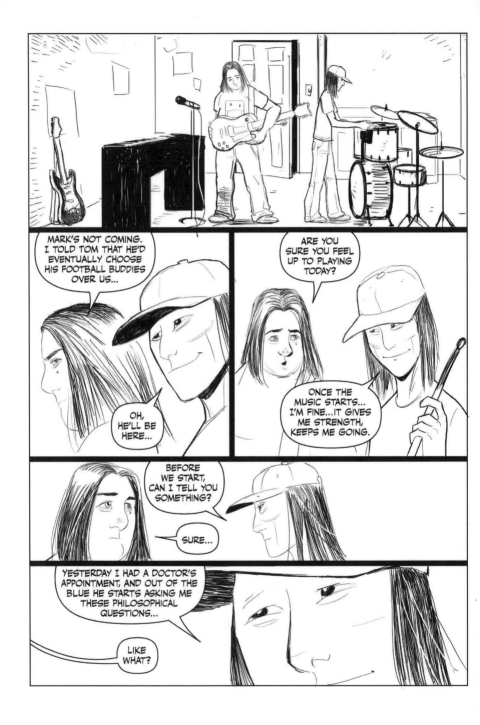

Chapter 10
Drive it Home

I. The Injustice Of Fear (Part Two)
II. In The End

RECOMMENDED LISTENING:

"WHATSERNAME"
GREEN DAY

Chapter 11
Jacoby's Last Stand

RECOMMENDED LISTENING:

"NERUDA"
TOM COCHRANE AND RED RIDER

"SINKING LIKE A SUNSET"
TOM COCHRANE

Chapter 12
Digital Black Epilogue

RECOMMENDED LISTENING:

"DIGITAL BLACK EPILOGUE"
URGE OVERKILL

"THE END"
THE BEATLES